1

THE LEGACY OF KENZO

WITHOUT TELLING YOU

MICHAEL ROBERSON

ILLUSTRATED BY DORIAN COTTEREAU

The Legacy of Kenzo: Without Telling You © 2016 by Michael Roberson

ISBN: 978-0-9973282-0-2

This book is a work of fiction. Names, characters, businesses, organizations, places, events and incidents either are the product of the author's imagination or are used fictitiously. Any resemblance to actual persons, living or dead, events or locales are entirely coincidental.

First Edition: June 2016

10 9 8 7 6 5 4 3 2 1

This book is dedicated to my daughters Asha and Kala.

Kenzo is from a royal family where his parents, Koumane` and Yonka, were king and queen of the land of Geneva. The people of Geneva were kidnapped by the looter gang. Kenzo was seven years old when he and his family fled their native land from the looters. Kenzo has two extraordinary powers that only his parents are aware of, indestructible skin, and supernatural strength, which he himself has not yet discovered. The Legacy of Kenzo begins....

After a long drive in the afternoon, Kenzo and his parents finally made it to the trick bike show. The bike riders were doing tricks that Kenzo had never seen before.

During the show, Kenzo got up and walked to the bathroom without telling his parents.

Kenzo turned the corner and, in front of him, he saw a bike with a note attached to it. He read the note out loud: "To my friend, Kenzo."

"Kenzo? Hey, that's me!" he said.

Kenzo was so excited, that he hopped on the bike, and put his feet on the pedals.

Kenzo started to ride his bike, but he stopped because there was

a huge crowd of people in front of him. "How can I get around

all these people?" he wondered.

Kenzo thought and thought, "Oh I know! I can say excuse me."

"Excuse me!" he said but the crowd did not move.

With a louder voice, he yelled "Excuse me please!" This time, the crowd heard him and moved over.

With an open lane, Kenzo could now ride his bike. "I want a bike like that mommy!" one of the children said with excitement.

Kenzo was happy because he was able to ride his bike through the crowd.

Just then, Kenzo heard a familiar voice calling his name, "Kenzo, Kenzo!" It was his mom and dad. They had a worried look on their face.

He quickly dropped his bike, and ran up to his parents.

"Kenzo, we are happy that we found you, but we are sad that you left without telling us. Always tell us where you are going so we know where you are. We need to protect you," Yonka said.

"I'm so sorry, Mom and Dad. I will never leave again without telling you," Kenzo said.

Relieved to be reunited with his parents, Kenzo still had a puzzling question:

"Dad, why did everyone move out of the way when I said excuse me?"

His dad replied proudly, "My son, you have the voice of a king, and whenever a King speaks, the people listen.

"I love you, Dad," Kenzo said

"I love you too, Kenzo," Koumane said.

Then they all walked back to finish watching the show.

To be continued...

Endorsements

This story gives a powerful message to children. Their voices have power. Kenzo's confidence comes from a strong foundation and validation of his parents. Kenzo "Without Telling You" is a story families can relate to.

-Tamika Thomas, Early Childhood Educator

A book with in depth meaning that will not only educate but be a tool to help youth get thru hard times. This book is a great animated manual for our youth who suffer from peer pressure and a lack of confidence in knowing they too can be great.

-Dawud Rawlings, Advocate/Entrepreneur/Mentor
Black Tie Mentoring & Young Gentlemen Group.

About the Author

My name is Michael Roberson. My two daughters, Asha and Kala are my inspiration for writing The Legacy of Kenzo.

I have been working with children since I was fifteen years old. I love being around them because they remind me to be free. Children naturally love and forgive. Too often as adults, we neglect to do these things on a daily basis.

I never thought I would be writing a children's book. One night I had a dream about a boy riding on a bike. I woke up, and wrote everything down because it sounded like an amazing story.

I want The Legacy of Kenzo to remind children to embrace their creativity, and to never be afraid to be who they are. A child's imagination is a terrible thing to waste.

www.ingramcontent.com/pod-product-compliance
Lightning Source LLC
Chambersburg PA
CBHW042209170626
46815CB00012B/256